JUNO VALENTINE
AND THE MAGICAL SHOES

WRITTEN BY
EVA CHEN

ILLUSTRATED BY
DEREK DESIERTO

FEIWEL AND FRIENDS · NEW YORK

A FEIWEL AND FRIENDS BOOK
An imprint of Macmillan Publishing Group, LLC
175 Fifth Avenue, New York, NY 10010

JUNO VALENTINE AND THE MAGICAL SHOES. Copyright © 2018 by Eva Chen. All rights reserved.
Printed in China by RR Donnelley Asia Printing Solutions Ltd., Dongguan City, Guangdong Province.

Our books may be purchased in bulk for promotional, educational, or business use.
Please contact your local bookseller or the Macmillan Corporate and Premium Sales Department
at (800) 221-7945 ext. 5442 or by e-mail at MacmillanSpecialMarkets@macmillan.com.

Library of Congress Control Number: 2018936437
ISBN 978-1-250-29726-6 (hardcover) / ISBN 978-1-250-20776-0 (ebook)

Book design by Carol Ly
Feiwel and Friends logo designed by Filomena Tuosto
First edition, 2018

1 3 5 7 9 10 8 6 4 2

mackids.com

FOR MY PARENTS,

WHO ALWAYS LET ME READ
AT THE DINING TABLE

It was just another Monday morning and, like most
Monday mornings, Juno Valentine was late for school.
This time, though, it was absolutely *not* her fault.

Her favorite shoes had vanished!

Juno's favorite shoes weren't particularly special.

They didn't light up. They didn't have wheels.

Compared to her friends' shoes,
they were pretty boring, actually.

But they were her favorite running-hopping-
skipping-muddy-puddle-jumping shoes.

Suddenly, Juno saw something twinkling at her
from the darkest, dustiest depths of her closet.

It was a cornucopia of shoes!

A feast of fashion!

Shoes everywhere just
waiting to be tried on!

Hello, Cleopatra!

¡Hola, Frida!

You know, thought Juno,
it'd really be a shame not to try
on *all* the shoes.

Juno stepped into
the shoes of . . .

QUEEN ELIZABETH I!   ANNA WINTOUR!   JANE GOODALL!

YAYOI KUSAMA!   OPRAH WINFREY!   GLORIA STEINEM!   LADY GAGA!   MARIE CURIE!

Cinderella's shoes weren't made for walking! Or skipping! Or anything fun for that matter.

But Serena's sneakers definitely were!
Game, set, match—victory was hers in
Serena's shoes.

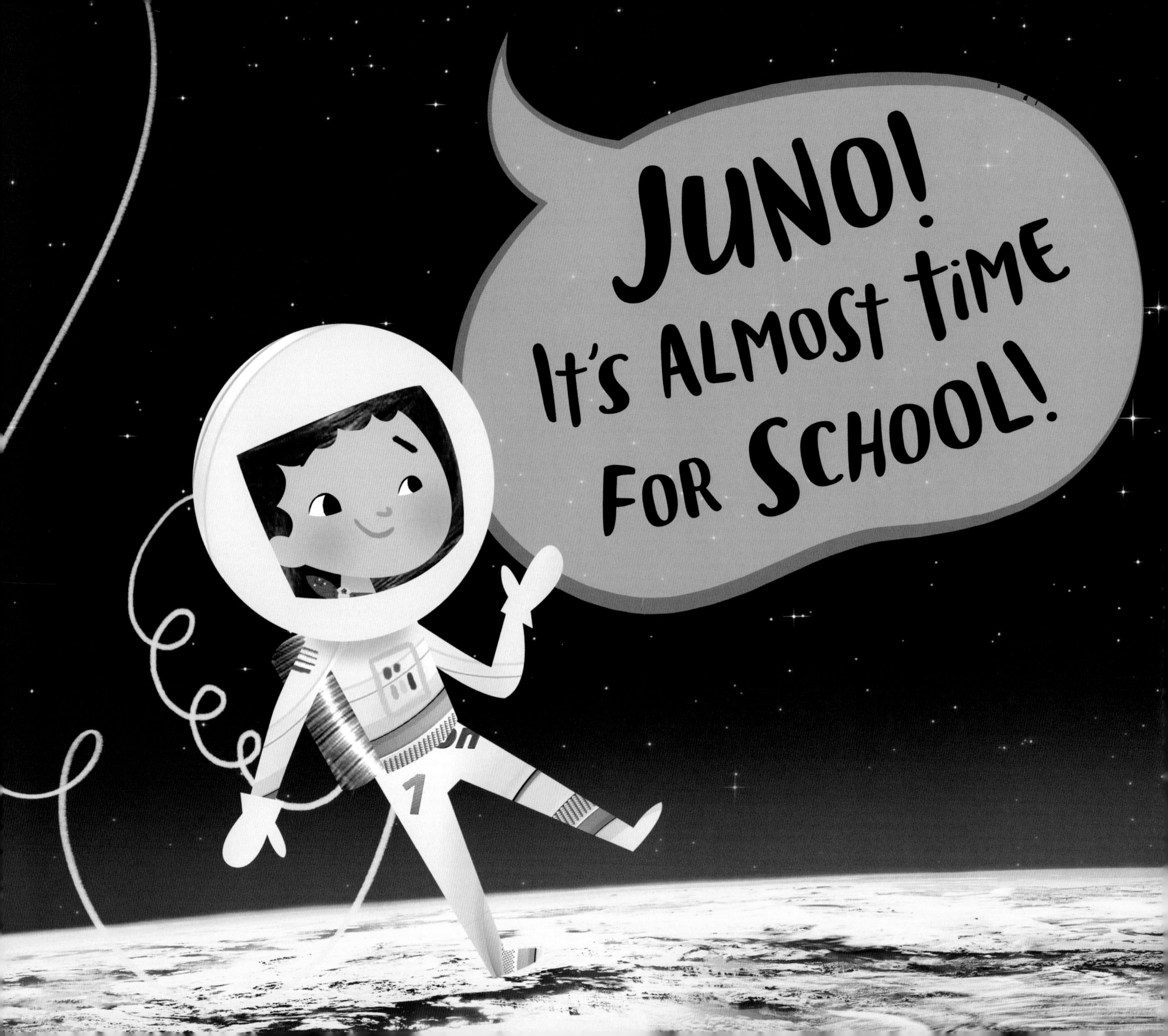
JUNO! It's ALMOST TIME FOR SCHOOL!

Juno felt major in Sally's moon boots but

she could hear her mom calling for her.

"Just one more pair, Mom!"

Once Juno started twirling in
Misty's ballet slippers, she couldn't stop!
Can't stop, won't stop twirling,
twirling, twirling, twirling . . .

SPLAT!

I wouldn't have gone SPLAT in my old shoes, thought Juno.

There they are!

Hooray!

Juno could finally
go home but, after she'd
been to the moon and back,
she had to admit her old
shoes seemed the teensiest
bit . . . boring.

Why not, thought Juno, add a little magic to my own shoes?

A splash of Frida's color!

A smidge of Misty's grace!

A dash of Gaga's sparkle!

And a heaping dollop of Serena's grit!

Now her shoes were the most un-boring shoes Juno had ever seen.

Juno was home!

And she was just in time.

THE END

JUNO'S GUIDE TO GROUNDBREAKING WOMEN (AND THEIR SHOES)

CLEOPATRA
Egyptian ruler (in addition to diplomat, naval commander, and linguist).

YAYOI KUSAMA
Japanese contemporary artist and sculptor known for her surreal and bold use of color.

CINDERELLA
Proved that nice girls can finish first (even in glass slippers).

FRIDA KAHLO
Mexican artist known for self-portraits, activism, and amazing eyebrow(s).

OPRAH WINFREY
American media mogul, actress, producer, philanthropist, giver-outer-of-cars.

SERENA WILLIAMS
American tennis legend with 23 Grand Slam titles and counting.

QUEEN ELIZABETH I
Queen of England and Ireland for 44 years; noted patron of the arts.

GLORIA STEINEM
American cofounder of *Ms. Magazine* who ushered in the feminist movement.

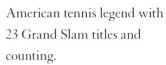

SALLY RIDE
Physicist, astronaut, and the first American woman to go into space.

ANNA WINTOUR
British editor-in-chief of *Vogue* magazine; fashion icon known to favor Prada.

LADY GAGA
American singer, songwriter, actress, and mother monster to millions of little monster fans worldwide.

MISTY COPELAND
Trailblazing ballerina—the first African American principal dancer in American Ballet Theater's history.

JANE GOODALL
British primatologist and anthropologist; world's top authority on chimpanzees.

MARIE CURIE
Polish physicist and chemist; first woman to win a Nobel Prize (and the first person and only woman ever to win twice).